Barnyard Tracks

by
Dee Dee Duffy

illustrated by
Janet Marshall

BELL BOOKS

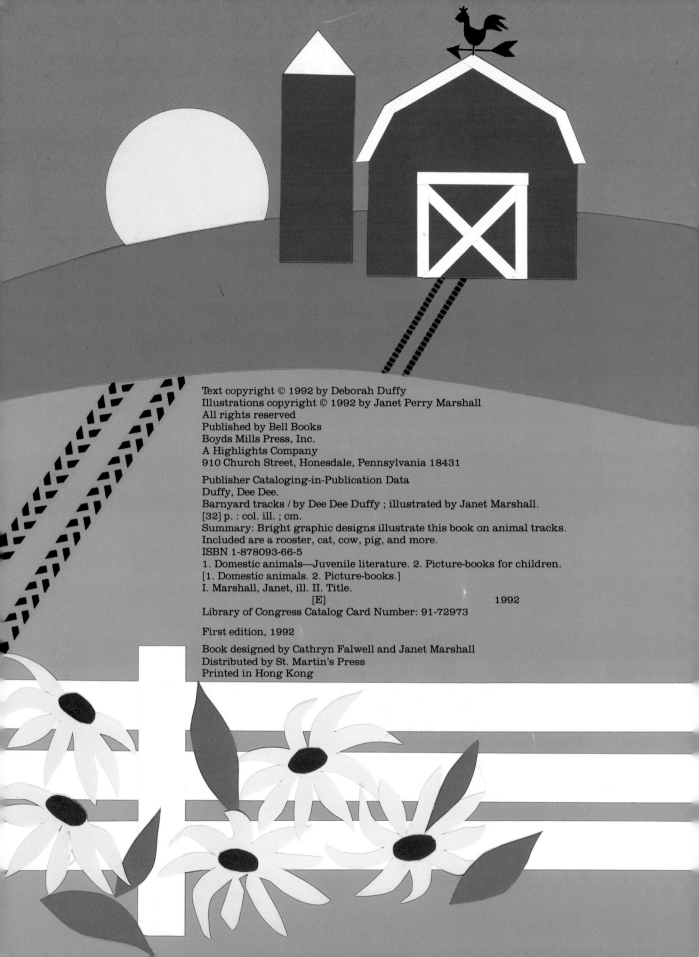

Text copyright © 1992 by Deborah Duffy
Illustrations copyright © 1992 by Janet Perry Marshall
All rights reserved
Published by Bell Books
Boyds Mills Press, Inc.
A Highlights Company
910 Church Street, Honesdale, Pennsylvania 18431

Publisher Cataloging-in-Publication Data
Duffy, Dee Dee.
Barnyard tracks / by Dee Dee Duffy ; illustrated by Janet Marshall.
[32] p. : col. ill. ; cm.
Summary: Bright graphic designs illustrate this book on animal tracks.
Included are a rooster, cat, cow, pig, and more.
ISBN 1-878093-66-5
1. Domestic animals—Juvenile literature. 2. Picture-books for children.
[1. Domestic animals. 2. Picture-books.]
I. Marshall, Janet, ill. II. Title.
[E]   1992
Library of Congress Catalog Card Number: 91-72973

First edition, 1992

Book designed by Cathryn Falwell and Janet Marshall
Distributed by St. Martin's Press
Printed in Hong Kong

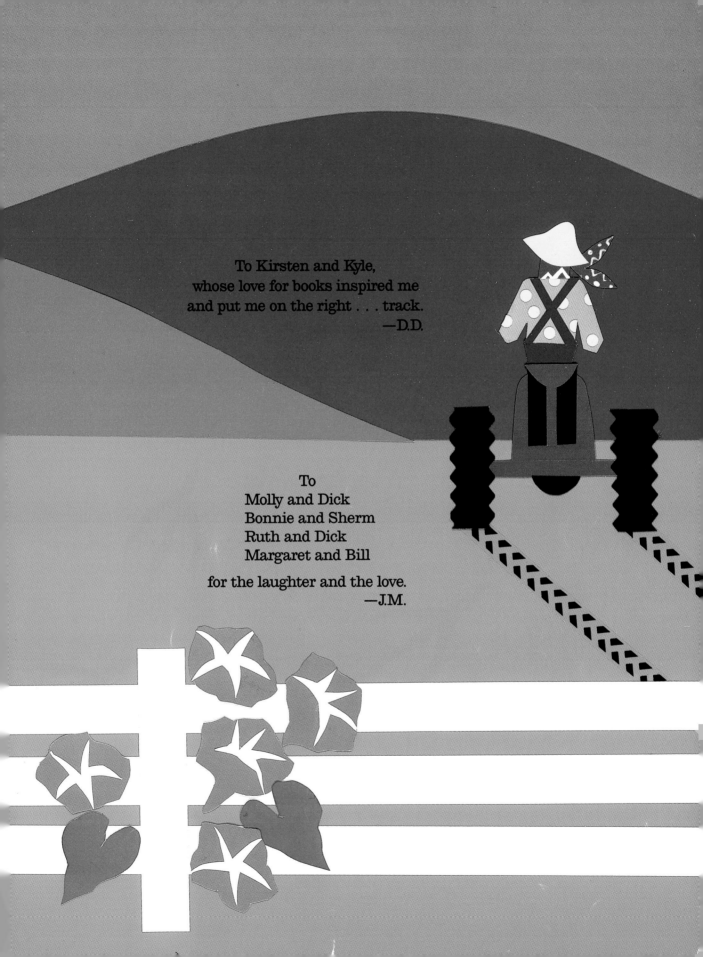

To Kirsten and Kyle,
whose love for books inspired me
and put me on the right . . . track.
—D.D.

To
Molly and Dick
Bonnie and Sherm
Ruth and Dick
Margaret and Bill

for the laughter and the love.
—J.M.

Look! I see some animal tracks.

Listen! I hear

cock-a-
doodle-
doo!

Who's there?

It's the
rooster.

Look! I see some animal tracks.

Listen ! I hear

oink ! oink !

Who's there?

It's the pigs.

Look! I see some animal tracks.

Listen! I hear

meow!

Who's there?

It's the cat.

Look! I see some animal tracks.

Listen ! I hear

quack!
quack!
splash!

Who's there?

It's the ducks.

Look! I see some
animal tracks.

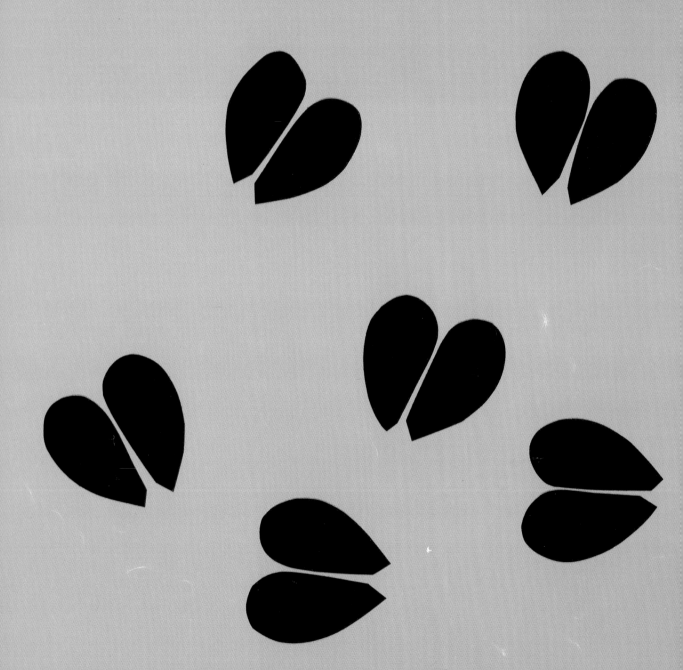

Listen! I hear

mooo!

Who's there?

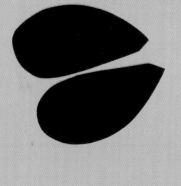
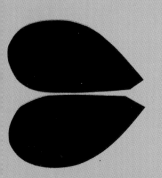

It's the cow.

Look! I see some
strange animal tracks.

Listen ! I hear

cock-a-doodle-doo!

quack!

meow!

What's happening ?

The fox is coming !

Look ! I see some big people tracks.

Listen! I hear

Who's there?

It's the farmer
scaring the
fox away.